The Lighthouse Keeper's Breakfast

Ronda and David Armitage

First published in 2000 by Scholastic Children's Books
This edition first published in 2014 by Scholastic Children's Books
Euston House, 24 Eversholt Street
London NW1 1DB
A division of Scholastic Ltd
www.scholastic.co.uk
London ~ New York ~ Toronto ~ Sydney ~ Auckland
Mexico City ~ Hong Kong

ISBN 978 1407 14438 2
Printed in China

1 3 5 7 9 10 8 6 4 2

The Lighthouse Keeper's Breakfast

Ronda and David Armitage

■SCHOLASTIC

M r and Mrs Grinling lived with their cat, Hamish, in a little white cottage perched high on the cliffs. Mr Grinling was a lighthouse keeper. By day and night, with his assistant Sam, he lovingly tended the light.

One Wednesday morning when Sam was polishing, he noticed a tiny inscription right at the top of the lighthouse. "Well, well," he said to himself. "Just fancy that!"

"Our lighthouse is 200 years old this year," he told everyone.

"We should celebrate," said Mrs Grinling.

"Maybe some presents," said Mr Grinling. "A fresh coat of red and white paint."

"And a party," said Mrs Grinling.

"How about fancy dress?" suggested Sally de la Croissant, the baker.

"Something to do with the sea," said Jason the postman. "I've got a lovely octopus suit."

"We can use my old sailing ship," roared Admiral Fleetabix,
"I'll moor her out in the bay."
"Can it be an all night party with a birthday breakfast?"
asked the children. "It is an extremely important occasion."
And everyone agreed that Mr and Mrs Grinling should
be the *Very Special Guests*.

NOTICE BOARD

THE LIGHTHOUSE
BIRTHDAY CELEBRATION
200 YEARS OLD

• VERY SPECIAL GUESTS: MR + MRS GRINLING

• ALL NIGHT SEA PARTY FOLLOWED BY
A BIRTHDAY BREAKFAST

• PLEASE WEAR FANCY DRESS

RSVP: SALLY DE LA
CROISSANT

It was so difficult to choose the best fancy dress.
"Shall I wear the shark suit?" asked Mr Grinling.
"Could I be a mermaid?" wondered Mrs Grinling.
But when they discovered the pirate costumes their
minds were quite made up.

"All my life I've yearned to be a pirate," sighed Mrs Grinling. "To spit and swear and roam the seven seas."
"And search for treasure on a treasure island," added Mr Grinling.
"We'll be splendid pirates," cried Mrs Grinling as she swashed and buckled around the room.
"Hattie and Herbert, the scourge of the seven seas."

"Oo-aargh!" said Mr Grinling and he swashed and buckled too.
"Perhaps Hamish could be our pirate cat," suggested Mrs Grinling.
But Hamish had very different ideas.

Whenever Mrs Grinling wanted him to try his pirate costume, Hamish disappeared.
"Drat that cat," she exclaimed.
"Where does he go these days?"

The Grinlings practised being pirates at every opportunity.

"I do want to be a pirate," he said sadly. "I'm just not very good at it. Perhaps I should have gone as a shark after all."

Mrs Grinling quite frightened Sam and the seagulls with her cursing and swearing.

On the night of the party the Grinlings rowed out towards the party ship.
At first its light shone clearly across the water but gradually they dimmed
and soon they vanished altogether.

"What can have happened, Mrs G?" said Mr Grinling. "We can't be lost." The waves slapped against the little boat. It was darker than Mr Grinling had ever seen it. And then as the lighthouse flashed across the bay . . .

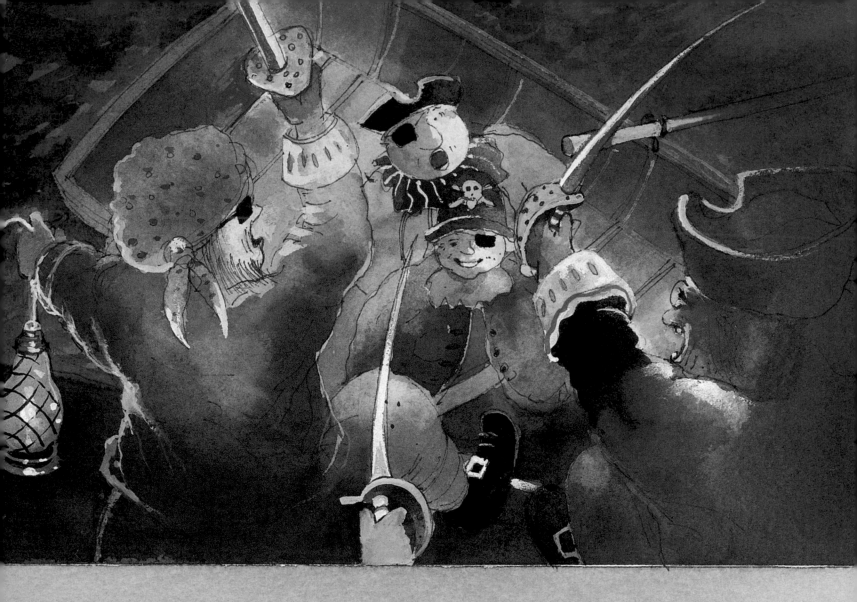

"Look, Mr G!" exclaimed Mrs Grinling. "Someone to rescue us."
A speed boat swished in beside them nearly swamping the little dinghy.
Three pirates leapt across the bow and thrust their shining cutlasses
in the air.
"Oo-aargh!" they roared and they rampaged round the dinghy.
Mrs Grinling was delighted.
"Real pirates," she whispered to Mr Grinling and she forgot all about
the Sea Party.

"Oo-aargh," growled the fiercest pirate. "We be pirates and this be our
pirate patch. We're on the look-out for likely new recruits."

"Oh, yes!" exclaimed Mrs Grinling. "We'd love to be pirates.
Yo-ho-ho and a bottle of rum."
Mr Grinling waved his cutlass rather feebly.
The pirates appeared rather surprised.
"'Course, you have to show us that you can be pirates,"
snarled the smallest and smelliest pirate.
"You have to pass the Incredibly Difficult Pirate Tests."
Mr Grinling wasn't sure about pirate tests.
"OK lads," shouted the fiercest pirate. "We'll blindfold 'em and gag 'em
and take 'em back to the Captain. She'll soon find out if they're made of
proper pirate material, you all know what she's like."

The pirate captain was a particularly nasty-looking piece of work.
She had black teeth and smelt of rotten fish and seaweed. A grubby
white parrot clung to her shoulder.
"Right, me hearties, what have we 'ere?" She peg-legged around the
Grinlings. "So you want to join our pirate crew?"

The Six Pirate Tests

"Oh yes, please," said Mrs Grinling.
"Definitely," agreed Mr Grinling.
"Well, you look like pirates and you smell like pirates but you have to pass the six pirate tests before you can be pirates. Are you ready?" asked the Captain. "So what comes first, me hearties?"

"The Swearing Test!" shouted the pirates.
Mrs Grinling swore loud and long.
The parrot covered his ears.
Mr Grinling thought for a while.
"Blithering bumbollards," he muttered at last.
The pirates shook their heads.

"Now the Sleeping in a Hammock in a Force Nine Gale Test.
Rock that ship, me bully boys and girls."
Mrs Grinling held tightly to the hammock sides and smiled happily.
Mr Grinling bounced right out of his hammock and was seasick
several times.
The pirates groaned.

"The Jolly Roger Flag Test," shouted Captain Bosibelle.
"Just a quick climb to the crow's-nest."
Mrs Grinling scampered up the rope ladder. At the top she not only
hoisted the flag but waved her cutlass.
"Shiver me timbers!" shouted the pirates.

Mr Grinling closed his eyes as he started to climb.
"Don't look down," he muttered to himself. "Think of Hamish and Sam.
Think of nice things to eat, Peach Surprise and iced sea biscuits, think
of-ah-ah-ah . . ."

He fell into a barrel of foul-smelling water.
"I'm so sorry," said the Captain.
"They're very polite for pirates," spluttered Mr Grinling to Mrs Grinling.

"Pirate Test number four," announced
Captain Bosibelle.
"Finding the Treasure," roared all of the pirates.
"Here's the map," said Captain Bosibelle.
"There's lovely treasure hidden on our ship,
you've got ten minutes to find it."
"Oo-aargh," shouted the Grinlings and off they raced.

OUTSIDE LOO

Off we go, Hattie –
not much time!

Up we go . . .

Quickly, Hattie . . .

Nothing here.

Oh dear!

This is empty.

CODE:
When all seems
All can be won.
A surprise awai
Under somebod

Herbert – I've
cracked the code!!

When all seems lost,
All can be won.
A surprise awaits,
Under somebody's . . .

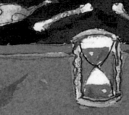

They found the treasure chest under
the bottom of a very small pirate.
"Open sesame!" shouted the pirates.
The chest was big enough for only one
jewel and two pieces of eight.
"We're a little short of treasure at the
moment," explained the Captain.
"No decent raids lately."

"And now the most dangerous, the most terrifying, the most dastardly test of them all."

"Eating Pirate Food!" shouted the pirates.

"Eating," said Mr Grinling happily. "Now eating is something I can do." Some of the smaller pirates sniggered.

Captain Bosibelle laid out the food. Two maggots and a weevil wriggled across the biscuit. Mrs Grinling turned quite green but Mr Grinling ate it, weevils, maggots and all.

"Hurrah," cheered the pirates.

"And now number six, the final test. If you pass this you can join our
pirate gang. Tell 'em, me bouncing buccaneers."

"Walking the Plank," cried the pirates.

"Oh," said Mrs Grinling.

"Dearie me," said Mr Grinling.

The water below looked smoothly dark and menacing. Mr Grinling
wished he was wearing the shark costume.

"Do you think I could ask for arm bands?" he whispered.

Mrs Grinling looked at the pirates' faces and shook her head.

"We've always wanted to be pirates, Mr G," she said. "We aren't
afraid of a little bit of water, are we?"
"Goodness, no," said Mr Grinling.
But his knees knocked and his tummy felt all wobbly like a jelly.
"Ready," he said and held his nose.
"Steady," said Mrs Grinling and she closed her eyes.
"Just a minute," said Mr Grinling, letting go of his nose.
"Something's amiss here. Whoever heard of new pirates walking the plank?
We could drown before we've done any pirating."

Suddenly the pirates pulled off their disguises.
"Surprise, surprise," they shouted.
The Grinlings were so astounded
they nearly fell into the water.
"Jason the postman!" exclaimed
Mr Grinling.

"Admiral Fleetabix!" cried
Mrs Grinling.
"And Sally de la Croissant!"
they said both together.

"We heard you longed to be pirates,"
she explained. "So we planned a
Pirate Experience. We had to be nasty
so you'd think we were real."
"We certainly did," said Mr Grinling
as he mopped his brow.

The lighthouse beamed its last light across the bay.
"It's party time," called Jason the postman.
He picked up his fiddle and started to play.
"May I have the pleasure, Pirate Herbert?" asked Mrs Grinling.
"Oo-aargh! Pirate Hattie," smiled Mr Grinling.
And they all danced until they could dance no more.

"Sun's up!" called Sally de la Croissant.
"Time for the birthday breakfast."
Mrs Grinling looked worried.
"We can't have the party without Hamish."
"Or Sam," said Mr Grinling.

"They're coming, they're coming!" shouted the children. "Just in time for the food," said Sam as he climbed on to the deck. He placed a large, wicker basket at the Grinlings' feet and carefully opened the lid.
Out jumped . . .

Hamish and Mrs Hamish and four little Hamishes.

"Now that's what I call real treasure," smiled Mrs Grinling.

Contents

About DiDA

DiDA (Diploma in Digital Applications) is a revolutionary series of qualifications launched by Edexcel in 2005, replacing GNVQ qualifications in ICT. As a suite of qualifications, it progresses from

- **Award** (AiDA), consisting of Module D201, to
- **Certificate** (CiDA), consisting of Module D201 plus one other module, to
- **Diploma** (DiDA), consisting of Modules D201 to D204.

Each unit requires 90 guided learning hours.

The qualification places emphasis on real-life skills. All assessment is 'paperless': you will submit an electronic portfolio of work via Edexcel Online for onscreen moderation. A Summative Project Brief (SPB), supplied each year by Edexcel via their website, will guide you through a series of tasks to be performed.

About Unit D201

D201 is the cornerstone of the qualification. You will gather information for your project work, analyse and present it, create paper and screen publications and present your work in an eportfolio. You will also learn to plan your project and to review and evaluate it once it is completed. This unit requires you to develop skills in many different areas of practical computing:

- Word processing and desktop publishing
- Spreadsheets
- Database software
- Presentation software
- Website software
- Artwork and imaging software

The structure of this book

Section 1 introduces a project brief similar in length, number of tasks and level of difficulty to the one set by Edexcel. By going through all the stages needed to complete the tasks in this sample project, you will gain the practical computing skills necessary to tackle the SPB. This section explains in detail how to plan your project, complete each task and create your eportfolio.

Section 2 is much shorter and contains chapters which you will find useful as you do your research work. These chapters can be covered at any time – don't leave them until you have completed Section 1!